W9-CBY-203

Dear Parent:
Your child's love of reading starts here!

Every child learns to read in a different way and at his or her own speed. Some go back and forth between reading levels and read favorite books again and again. Others read through each level in order. You can help your young reader improve and become more confident by encouraging his or her own interests and abilities. From books your child reads with you to the first books he or she reads alone, there are I Can Read Books for every stage of reading:

SHARED READING
Basic language, word repetition, and whimsical illustrations, ideal for sharing with your emergent reader

BEGINNING READING
Short sentences, familiar words, and simple concepts for children eager to read on their own

READING WITH HELP
Engaging stories, longer sentences, and language play for developing readers

READING ALONE
Complex plots, challenging vocabulary, and high-interest topics for the independent reader

ADVANCED READING
Short paragraphs, chapters, and exciting themes for the perfect bridge to chapter books

I Can Read Books have introduced children to the joy of reading since 1957. Featuring award-winning authors and illustrators and a fabulous cast of beloved characters, I Can Read Books set the standard for beginning readers.

A lifetime of discovery begins with the magical words **"I Can Read!"**

Visit www.icanread.com for information
on enriching your child's reading experience.

 flowers

 pony

 garden

 present

 kite

 recipe

 lemons

 sand castle

 photo

 scrapbook

 ponies

 table

I Can Read!

BEGINNING
1
READING

A
Secret
Gift

by Ruth Benjamin author

illustrated by Gayle Middleton

colors

HarperCollins*Publishers*

Daisy Jo was a happy .

She loved working _unicorn_

in her  . _garden_

She loved the smell

of her  . _flowers_

Most of all, she loved

doing nice things

for her  friends.

unicorns

Butterscotch wanted to thank

Daisy Jo for being

such a great friend.

"I will make a !"

said Butterscotch.

Book

"The other  can add

to the .

When it is finished, we will

surprise Daisy Jo with it!"

making a book for Daisy Jo

Butterscotch called a meeting
name (handwritten)

in the Café. — *eat food* (handwritten)

The   liked the idea!

"I will add a [picture] to the [book]," said Fluttershy.
picture (handwritten)

"This [picture] of Daisy Jo
picture (handwritten)

and me making a [sand castle]
sand castle (handwritten)

at the beach is perfect."

meeting to make a book (handwritten)

8

"I will add dried

to the ,"

said Star Swirl.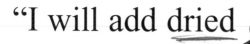

"Daisy Jo and I both

love .

Daisies are her favorite,

of course!"

"I will add Daisy Jo's

favorite cupcake —recipe

to the  ,"

said Sweetberry.

"Daisy Jo likes cupcakes with

 and chocolate chips.

Yummy!"

Just Daisy Jo likes

Just then, Daisy Jo walked in.

She saw the  hard at work.

"What are you doing?" she asked.

Butterscotch hid the

under the ☐.

"It is a surprise!" said Butterscotch.

"Meet us tonight at the Café

to find out what it is."

almost get
caught

"A surprise," said Daisy Jo

to herself.

"My birthday is soon. . . .

Are the making me an

early birthday ?"

she wondered out loud.

"What could it be?

Maybe a ?

Or a poem?"

Back at her house,

Butterscotch looked at the .

She added a drawing

of Daisy Jo in her .

"This is filled

with good memories.

Daisy Jo will love it!"

Butterscotch said.

That night, the  met

at the Café.

When Daisy Jo walked through

the door, the  shouted,

"Surprise!"

"We made this for you,

Daisy Jo," said Butterscotch.

"We wanted to thank you for

being such a great friend."

"Wow!" said Daisy Jo.

"I tried to guess what the

surprise would be!"

Daisy Jo was happy.

The were the greatest

friends she could ever ask for.

"Thank *you* for being

such wonderful

friends," Daisy Jo said.

"I love my .

It is the best surprise ever!"